NOW YOU SEE ME
NOW YOU DON'T

Patricia Hegarty

Jonny Lambert

LiTTLE TiGER

LONDON

I am **Chameleon.**
I do as I please.
I can play tricks
and nobody sees.

Just look at old **Big Ears,**
she thinks I'm a rock . . .

But once in a while,
I just HAVE to go . . .

BOO!

So watch out, dear reader . . .
I might come for YOU!

There's a horrified gasp
as all turn to see . . .
But Frog's disappeared –
all eyes are on ME!

Frog turned the tables
and now I can see:
It isn't so funny
when the joke is on me.

My camouflage tricks
are a thing of the past,
And everything's peaceful
in the jungle, at last . . .

How do I do it?
It's **easy** as pie.

I can **change colour**
in the blink of an eye.

When work's to be done,
I just disappear.

Chores are for **bores**,
not for me – oh, no fear!

If I fancy a snack,
I just take my pick.
I **LOVE** a banana –
look at this trick!

There's fun to be had
with this **feathery** pair . . .

I didn't do it!
I wasn't there!

I'm feeling INVINCIBLE!
Now what shall I do?
A sloth, fast asleep?
It's too good to be true!

TICKLE
TICKLE

Wheee! Down he goes,
with a bump and a lurch . . .
And bounces Anteater
right off of his perch.

Tee-hee, poor fellow,
look at him go!

He's going to land . . .

. . . on Jaguar!
UH-OH.

No, thank you, Chameleon.
Your pranks are not cool.
Let's see how you feel
when it's YOU who's the fool . . .

A stone that
can talk?

BOO!

That gave her a
shock!

For Oliver Thomas ~ P H

For Imogen, the new kid on the block ~ J L

LITTLE TIGER PRESS LTD,
an imprint of the Little Tiger Group
1 Coda Studios,
189 Munster Road,
London SW6 6AW
www.littletiger.co.uk

First published in Great Britain 2020

Text by Patricia Hegarty
Text copyright © Little Tiger Press Ltd 2020
Illustrations copyright © Jonny Lambert 2020
Jonny Lambert has asserted his right to be identified as the illustrator
of this work under the Copyright, Designs and Patents Act, 1988
A CIP catalogue record for this book is available from the British Library

2 4 6 8 10 9 7 5 3 1